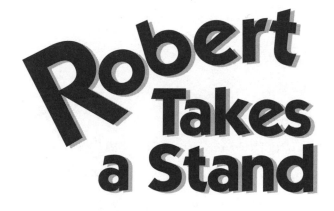

Also by Barbara Seuling

Oh No, It's Robert

Robert and the Great Pepperoni

Robert and the Weird & Wacky Facts

Robert and the Back-to-School Special

Robert and the Lemming Problem

Robert and the Great Escape

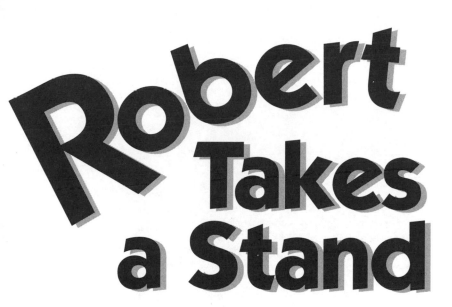

Robert Takes a Stand

by Barbara Seuling
Illustrated by Paul Brewer

Cricket Books
Chicago

Library of Congress Cataloging-in-Publication Data

Seuling, Barbara.
  Robert takes a stand / by Barbara Seuling ; illustrated by Paul
Brewer.— 1st ed.
      p. cm.
Summary: Political experience gained in a class election comes in handy
when Robert and his friend Paul act on behalf of endangered animals.
  ISBN 0-8126-2712-1 (cloth : alk. paper)
  [1. Schools—Fiction. 2. Grandmothers—Fiction. 3. Endangered
animals—Fiction.] I. Brewer, Paul, 1950- ill. II. Title.
  PZ7.S5135Rq 2004
  [Fic]—dc22
                                                        2003018499

For the five Antonellis

Heather
John
Phil
Jennifer
Joanna

—B. S.

For Dr. Jeffrey Ninberg

—P. B.

Contents

The Clouded Leopard

"Mom! Mom!" Robert burst into the house like a small explosion.

Huckleberry ran on his fat little puppy legs to greet him. Robert scooped up the wiggly dog and nuzzled him as he looked around. "Where's Mom, Huck?"

Robert's mom came dashing down the stairs. "What's wrong?" she asked.

Robert put Huckleberry down. The puppy started chewing on his shoelaces.

"Nothing's wrong," said Robert. "I just got picked to be a clouded leopard!"

"Slow down, Robert," said Mrs. Dorfman. "What's a clouded leopard? And why were you picked to be one?"

Robert pulled his foot gently from Huckleberry's grasp. He slipped his backpack off and opened the zipper.

"It's this," he said, pulling out a picture. He showed it to his mom. "It's a leopard with these amazing spots that look like little clouds," said Robert. "Everyone gets to be an endangered animal and has to do a report on it. I want to dress up as one. Can you make me a costume to look like this, Mom?" Robert took a second to breathe. "Can you?"

Mrs. Dorfman seemed to swallow hard. "I . . . I . . . Can't we buy one?" she said.

Robert knew they would never find a clouded leopard costume. He'd have to think of something else.

"That's O.K., Mom. Never mind." He got up to go, grabbing his backpack. He motioned for Huckleberry to follow.

"Wouldn't you like a glass of milk or juice?" asked his mom.

"No, thanks," said Robert, running up the stairs. Huckleberry bumbled along beside him. "I have to get started on my homework."

Robert's room was cluttered with all his hobbies. First, there were his animals.

He had his turtledoves, Flo and Billie, in a birdcage on his bookcase.

Beside the birdcage was a plastic case that contained a huge, hairy tarantula named Fuzzy.

Next to his bed there was a soft bed for Huckleberry. The puppy never slept in his dog bed because he slept with Robert, but it was there, just in case. It was filled with dog toys.

Then there were Robert's collections. Robert had a row of Weird & Wacky Facts books on his bookshelf.

He had rocks from every place he or his family had ever been.

He had jelly jars with interesting things he'd found in Van Saun Park. One was a tiny G.I. Joe combat boot. Some kid must have lost it by the duck pond.

And he had his plastic dinosaurs, lined up according to size on the windowsill.

In the center of Robert's room was his beanbag chair. He sat in it to think. Sometimes his best friend, Paul, sat in it with him when they had to think together.

Robert lifted Huckleberry and sat in the beanbag chair with him. "I want to do something special for my report," he told the puppy. The cuddly puppy sniffed at Robert's ear.

"A costume would have been great."
Robert sighed. "What else can I do?"

Huckleberry licked Robert's cheek.

Laughing, Robert held up his hands in front of his face and peeked through his fingers. "Hey, great idea, Huck!" he exclaimed. "I'll make a mask!"

"Pop-ee-ay Mashay"

Thumping downstairs with Huckleberry at his heels, Robert went to the kitchen cabinet and took out a mixing bowl. Then he went to the flour canister and scooped some flour into the bowl.

Ms. Valentine, the art teacher, had showed Robert's class how to make masks with something called "papier-mâché." Except she pronounced it funny, like "pop-ee-ay mashay."

Carefully, Robert climbed the stairs, carrying the bowl of flour. "Don't trip me,

Huckleberry," he said. In the bathroom, he poured water over the flour until it got sticky and gooey. In his room again, he put the bowl on his desk.

He needed lots of newspaper. He and Huckleberry thumped downstairs again.

He had almost all of last Sunday's *Star-Ledger* in his arms when his dad came in.

"Hi, Tiger," he said. "How's it going?"

Robert's father often called him "Tiger." Robert thought it was because his dad wished Robert were more of an athlete, like his brother, Charlie.

"Hi, Dad. Fine," he said.

"What are the newspapers for?"

"A mask," said Robert.

"He's going to be a clouded leopard," said his mom, coming out of the kitchen with a steaming mug of tea in her hand.

While his mom explained to his dad what a clouded leopard was, Robert and

Huckleberry thundered back upstairs.

Robert looked at the picture. First, he needed a round shape. A soccer ball would be good, but he didn't have a soccer ball. Charlie had a basketball. Maybe he could borrow it. No, he'd better not even ask.

He looked under his bed. There was a lego piece, a sock, a chew toy and—just what he needed—a balloon he had never blown up.

Robert blew up the balloon and made a knot in it. Huckleberry watched, his tail wagging. "This isn't for you, Huckleberry," he told the puppy. He handed Huckleberry a squeaky chew toy from the dog bed instead.

He spread out some of the newspaper on the floor and cut strips from the rest. He soaked the strips in the bowl with the flour paste mixture.

When the paper was good and wet, he laid it across one side of the balloon and

smoothed it out. He waited for the strips
to dry, touching them every few minutes.
In between he played with Huckleberry.

He did several layers. They took a long
time to dry. Finally, he decided to start his

homework so he could stop fussing with the wet strips. The squeaks from Huckleberry's toy, as he played with it, made Robert smile.

When his mom called him to dinner, Robert checked the mask. It was still wet. Huckleberry had fallen asleep, his chew toy next to him. Robert tiptoed out of the room, letting him sleep. He would be back later to finish up. He washed his hands in the bathroom and went downstairs to dinner.

Protectors of the Earth

They sat around the dinner table while his mom filled their plates from the big pot. On Robert's plate she put one large lump and two small ones, covered with gravy.

"Well, Tiger, what about this project of yours?" asked his dad.

"We have to study about endangered animals," said Robert. "Mrs. Bernthal says it's our job to protect the earth and all its creatures."

"What do you have to learn about these animals?" his dad asked.

"About how they live, I guess." Robert stabbed the large brown lump with his fork.

"And how they die!" added Charlie.

Robert didn't think that was funny, even though it was true.

"Charlie . . ." said Mrs. Dorfman.

"It's true, Mom," said Charlie. "Elephants, rhinos . . . lots of animals die because people want their tusks or horns. I saw it on TV. They even club baby seals to death just to get their fur!"

Robert felt his stomach flip. "They do not!" he protested. Charlie was always teasing him. This sounded like another of his teases. He looked at his dad for him to agree. But his dad didn't say anything.

"Oh," said his mom, "I have good news! Your grandmother is coming to visit."

Robert was grateful to his mom for changing the subject. She knew how he felt about animals. He tried to cut the lump on his fork with his knife.

"Really?" said Charlie. "When?"

"On Friday," said Mrs. Dorfman. "She'll be here when you get home from school."

Robert loved Grandma Judy. It's true she smoked too much. His father wrinkled his nose whenever she lit up a cigarette, so she went outside in the yard to smoke. But Grandma Judy made them laugh, and she always brought presents for him and Charlie.

Robert's knife slid off the lump as he sawed away and splashed gravy across the table. "Oops!" he said.

"That knife must be dull," said his mom, jumping up. She got a wet cloth and wiped the table.

Robert pushed the lump off his fork and ate the smaller one instead. What was it— a potato? He had no idea.

Last time Grandma Judy visited, she brought Robert a glow-in-the-dark poster of Jurassic Park because she knew he liked dinosaurs. It was so terrifying, he couldn't sleep, so he rolled it up and put it in his closet. He would have to take it out and put it up when Grandma Judy was here. He didn't want to hurt her feelings. He would just have to remember not to look at the poster before he went to bed at night.

After dinner, Robert ran upstairs to finish his mask.

"Oh no!" he cried as he went into his room. The bowl with the flour paste mixture was upside down, and Huckleberry was licking the paste off the newspapers. Robert grabbed the puppy and ran downstairs.

"Mom! Dad! Huckleberry ate my paste!" he cried. "He's poisoned!"

"It was just flour and water, right?" asked his mom.

Robert nodded, his heart beating rapidly.

"He may have a bellyache," said his dad, "but he'll be O.K. You're going to have to be more careful, Tiger. Puppies think everything is food."

Robert kept an eye on Huckleberry as he cleaned up the mess. That was a close call. He didn't know what he'd do if anything happened to his puppy.

His mask seemed to be O.K. Robert felt it. It was still damp, but he could finish it tomorrow. He put it up high on his dresser so Huckleberry couldn't reach it.

As he got ready for bed, Robert thought again about what Charlie had said. He squeezed toothpaste onto his toothbrush. As he brushed, Robert couldn't help thinking about those baby seals. He spat into the sink.

He remembered a report he once did on sea turtles. They swallowed plastic bags that floated in the water, thinking they were food. Many of them died. Maybe every animal was in danger of something. And maybe he could figure out a way to help them.

Auntie Fur

At Paul's house after school, Robert and Paul did their homework together.

Robert sat at Paul's computer, clicking on Web site after Web site. He found out a lot of animals were in danger. They were hunted for their tusks or horns or fur—not even for food.

"Look at this!" he cried out. Paul rolled off the bed and came over to see. It was a Web site about hunting baby seals. A series of photos showed the friendly seals coming up to greet the hunters, who then clubbed them to death.

Paul looked on, horrified.

"I thought Charlie was teasing me," said Robert. "But it's true!"

They continued to read together.

Robert pulled up a page on the clouded leopard. It showed the spots that looked like little clouds.

"It's beautiful," said Paul.

"Yeah," said Robert, "but it says here it's being hunted for its unusual fur." Robert printed out the page.

"Did you see *101 Dalmatians?*" he asked Paul.

"Yeah!" said Paul. "Cruella De Vil—she was scary—wanted to make a coat out of those little puppies. That was a great movie."

"Yeah," Robert agreed sadly, moving aside to give Paul a turn.

Paul clicked away.

"There's a group called Greenpeace," he said. "They go in boats and stop the hunters."

"Really?" said Robert. "That's cool."

"Yeah," agreed Paul.

"Here's something about an anti-fur group."

"Who's Auntie Fur?" asked Robert.

"It's not a person," said Paul, laughing. "It's a group. They are against killing animals for their fur."

"We should do what they do," said Robert.

"I don't think so," said Paul. "They spray-paint fur coats whenever they see them—even when they're on people!"

"No!" said Robert. "I wouldn't do that. Besides, my parents would kill me."

"But look! It says they also carry signs outside stores that sell fur," added Paul, still looking at the computer screen.

"We could do that," said Robert. "The signs would tell people why it's wrong to wear fur coats. Then they won't go in and buy them. We can ask some kids in our class to do it with us."

"Won't we get in trouble?" asked Paul

"I don't know," said Robert. "But we have to do something to save these animals!"

That night, Robert woke up in a terrible fright. He had been dreaming. Cruella De Vil was running after Huckleberry, waving a knife. Huck kept tumbling and falling and Cruella was getting closer and closer to him.

Robert went back to sleep with Huckleberry wrapped in his arms.

Bingo!

By three o'clock on Friday, the whole class had heard about the anti-fur protest and wanted to be part of it. The plan was set.

A week from tomorrow, on Saturday morning, they would meet at the mall. They would make signs to carry telling people why they shouldn't buy fur coats. They would carry their signs as they marched up and down in front of Fancy Furs, a store. As the bell rang, they were still talking about it.

When Robert opened the door to his house, he knew Grandma Judy was there. He smelled her perfume. It was like a flower garden.

"Is that my sweet Robert?" he heard from the kitchen. He ran in, dropping his backpack behind him.

"Grandma Judy!" he cried, wrapping his arms around her as far as they would go. His mom smiled from across the table.

Grandma Judy smothered him with kisses. "How are you?" she asked. "You have grown so tall since I last saw you, I hardly recognized you." Grandma Judy always said that.

Huckleberry tried to scramble up Robert's pants leg. "I'm fine," said Robert, picking up the puppy and holding him up. "Look, Grandma Judy, I got a puppy! His name is Huckleberry."

"Well, it's about time," Grandma Judy said,

winking at Robert's mom. She reached into a big canvas bag next to her chair and took out a hard rubber bone and put it on the floor. "So hello, Huckleberry," she said, patting the dog's head.

Robert put Huckleberry down to play with his new bone.

Grandma Judy reached into the bag again and took out a cloth doll. She handed it to Robert. He stared at it.

"It's not for you, silly. It's for the puppy."

A doll for a dog? Grandma Judy seemed to read Robert's mind.

"The store said the bone would be good for a puppy's teeth," she said. "But I think he needs something else, too. The doll is for when he needs something soft. You'll see. He'll love it to pieces." How did Grandma know so much about dogs?

"I had a dog once, too, you know," she said, reading his mind again.

"Your mother told me about your puppy," Grandma Judy said. "And I remembered how my little Skippy loved his doll." Robert dropped it to the floor next to Huckleberry.

Charlie came in. "Hi, Grandma Judy." He kissed her, and Grandma Judy grabbed him in a big hug and kissed him back.

"Look how you've grown!" she said. "These boys are going to be taller than me, soon."

"Mom," said Robert's mother, "Charlie has been taller than you for two years already. Stand up. You'll see how tall he is."

"Never mind," said Grandma Judy. "I'll see soon enough." Grandma Judy was really short, but she did not like to be teased about it.

Then she grabbed the handles on the canvas bag, lifted it up, and dumped it out on the table.

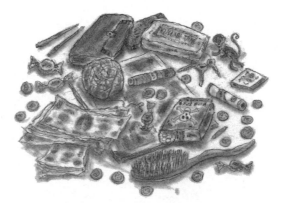

Among the hairbrush, lipstick, pack of cigarettes, book of matches, wallet, little pocket pack of tissues, small black address book, ball of green wool, crochet hook, keys, several hard candies, a magazine, two pens, and Grandma Judy's lucky charm—a plastic monkey that Robert had given her when he was five years old—was money. Lots and lots of money.

"Wow!" was all Robert could say.

"This is from bingo," she said. "I've been having a lucky streak."

Mom laughed. "It couldn't be because you buy ten cards at once, could it?"

Robert had heard about Grandma Judy
playing bingo every week at the senior
center. He had no idea she played for
money.

"I don't know how much is there," she
said. "You and Charlie get to count it—then

you and Charlie get to keep it." Immediately, the boys scrambled for the money. At the sudden movement, Huckleberry came running to see what was going on.

"You'll split it fifty-fifty, of course," she added. They slowed down.

Robert started to count, but his brother was faster, so he let Charlie do it. While Charlie counted it a second time, to be sure, Robert reached for Huckleberry's ball and rolled it for him. The puppy bounced after it.

Charlie made piles of ten-, five-, and one-dollar bills, plus three stacks of quarters.

"There's one hundred and seventy-six dollars, Grandma Judy," Charlie said.

"Wonderful," she said. "Now you are rich men."

Robert's mom laughed. "That's a lot of money," she said. "Maybe you should put it away for something special."

"I know something special I'm going to buy with my money," Charlie announced.

"What's that?" asked his mother.

"A new skateboard," he said. "I saw it at the sports store. It glows in the dark."

"You don't go skateboarding at night," his mom reminded him.

"I know, but I think it's neat," Charlie said.

Robert was still trying to figure out how much money each of them would get. He'd put his in his frog bank. He had been saving up a long time for a computer. This would speed things up a little.

Mr. Dorfman came into the room. "I'm going for the pizza," he announced. "Any special requests?"

"The usual," said Mrs. Dorfman. "Don't forget some with pepperoni for Robert."

Family Stories

While his dad was out, the rest of Robert's family caught up on family news.

Grandma Judy talked about poor Mrs. Restivo, an old family friend, dying suddenly of a heart attack.

Robert lay on the floor, scratching Huckleberry behind his ears.

"And what do you think about Becky Weinstein getting engaged?" Grandma Judy said, a big smile on her face.

Robert didn't know who Becky Weinstein was. His mom must have known her because she smiled. "Yes," she said. "Isn't it nice?"

Mom reported that her travel agency business was doing really well. Robert wondered why his mom liked her job so much. She made vacation plans for everyone else, but the Dorfmans hardly ever went on family vacations.

Charlie told Grandma Judy about his team winning the hockey championship. He was recounting various football victories when the front door opened.

Whew! That was close. Robert was glad he didn't have to hear Charlie cover every sport he played. He didn't think there was enough time in one day.

"I had an idea on the way home," said Mr. Dorfman, boxes piled in his arms. He kicked the door closed behind him. Huckleberry ran to greet him.

Mr. Dorfman placed the pizza boxes on the coffee table, where Mrs. Dorfman had laid out placemats. "Instead of a regular movie, we can show Grandma Judy the video of our trip to Great Adventure."

Robert reached over and grabbed Huckleberry just as the bouncy puppy discovered the food.

"Great!" shouted Charlie. "Grandma Judy, wait'll you see us way up on the roller coaster. If you listen, you can hear Robert scream!"

"Can not!" said Robert, hanging on to Huckleberry. He had not screamed, but he had thought he was going to die. He didn't think you could tell that in the video.

Dad put the tape in the VCR, and they helped themselves to pizza.

Robert shared his slice with Huckleberry.

After the Great Adventure video, and one of Robert in his Dracula costume for

Halloween, there was another showing an old man walking across the yard with a toddler holding on to his index finger.

"That was Charlie's sixth birthday party," said his mom. "See him over there riding his new bike? And that's Grandpa Aaron, Robert, teaching you to walk."

Robert never knew his grandfather, who died when Robert was just a baby. He was too young to remember the scene in the video.

Grandma Judy got a little teary. "Grandpa liked only pepperoni on his pizza, like you," she told Robert.

"Really?" said Robert. That made him feel better. At least he felt a connection now to the older man in the video.

"It's great to remember old times," Grandma Judy said. She turned to Robert and Charlie. "But you children are young. You are still creating your memories."

Robert yawned. It was getting late, and he had to take Huckleberry out in the yard one more time. The puppy was just about housebroken, but Robert didn't want to take any chances.

He would have to wait until tomorrow to tell Grandma Judy about his project and the protest.

Shocked

On Saturday morning, Robert got dressed quickly.

"C'mon, Huck," he said. He bounced downstairs with the puppy at his heels.

His dad and Charlie weren't down yet. "Hi, Mom. Hi, Grandma Judy," he said.

"Good morning, Robert," said his mom.

"Good morning, handsome," Grandma Judy said.

Robert let Huckleberry out into the yard and sat down at the kitchen table. He poured some Raisin Explosion cereal into his bowl.

"So how are you doing in school?" asked Grandma Judy.

"Gfff," he answered, his mouth full of cereal.

"You have a nice teacher?"

Robert nodded. "Mffss wuffstufff," he answered. He stopped to chew and swallow. Then he continued. "Mrs. Bernthal. She's really nice. She bought us a snake for our classroom."

"She bought you a snake?" Grandma Judy made a face.

"She's really great, Grandma Judy. Her name is Sally, and she's green." Robert took a sip of juice.

"Your teacher is green?"

"No!" Robert laughed, spraying juice across the table. "The snake, Grandma Judy!"

"Boy oh boy oh boy," said Grandma Judy. "School wasn't like that in my day."

"And you know what else, Grandma Judy?" Robert said. He knew she would like hearing about his endangered animal project and especially about the anti-fur protest.

"Maybe you'd better finish your juice now and tell Grandma Judy on the way," his mom interrupted. "We're going to the mall, and I'd like you to come with us."

"O.K.," said Robert, wiping up his juice with the dish cloth. "How come?"

Robert often stayed home by himself. He had planned on finishing his mask. He still had to paint it and cut out eyeholes.

"Because we may be a while—and Grandma Judy wants to go to Smilin' Jack's for lunch." She smiled. "We thought you'd like to come along."

Smilin' Jack's! Robert looked at Grandma Judy. She grinned. It was his favorite restaurant, and it had become hers, too, when she came to visit.

Robert was the one who first told Grandma Judy about it. He knew she would like the old-fashioned decor of the restaurant. There were comic strips and movie posters on the walls. Old TV commercials, in black and white, played on TVs placed around the room.

Once, while they were there, they saw an old cereal commercial, and Grandma Judy told him how she and her brother had talked their parents into buying many different cereals just to get the prizes they had inside or to save the box tops for bigger prizes.

"We had so much cereal, we could have opened a store!" she had said, laughing.

"There were prizes in your cereal?" Robert had asked.

"Oh my, yes," Grandma Judy had said. "Pins with pictures of our favorite comics characters, cards with secret codes on them, and little figures. We collected them all. And if you saved up enough box tops and sent them in, you could get rings with whistles or secret decoders in them."

Robert wished his cereal had something interesting in it besides raisins. Robert brought his bowl and glass over to the sink and then let Huckleberry in.

They were getting ready to leave. Robert poured puppy food into Huckleberry's bowl and put fresh water in his water dish.

"Good-bye, Huck," he said. "We'll be back soon. Now you be good," he reminded the puppy. He put on his jacket and waited outside.

The garage door opened, and his mom backed the car out of the garage. Grandma Judy was already in the front seat, her seat belt fastened.

Robert climbed into the backseat and looked at his grandmother in shock.

She was wearing a fur coat!

Public Enemy #1

Robert was so surprised, he didn't know what to say or do. He just sat back as his mom and Grandma Judy chattered away.

As he stared at the fur wrapped around his grandmother, Robert's mind raced. *What kind of animal is that, anyway? Does Grandma Judy know how many of them got killed to make that coat? She's the kind of person the anti-fur people hate! What if someone from his class saw him walking next to a fur coat?*

"Can I wait in the car?" Robert asked, as they pulled into a spot in the parking lot.

"No, Robert, you may not," said his mom.

Rats! Maybe if he had said "May I" instead of "Can I" his mom would have let him.

As they got out of the car, Robert leaned back in to open the glove compartment. He took out a pair of sunglasses his dad had left there. He put them on.

"Robert, you're being weird," his mom said.

"Oh, let him be," said Grandma Judy. "All the children dress in costumes these days. Haven't you noticed?"

She motioned with her head to a couple of girls passing by. One had on purple striped pants and the other wore earrings that could almost be Christmas tree ornaments.

"I guess so," Robert's mom said, laughing.

Robert walked a long way ahead of his mom and his grandmother.

He tried to duck whenever he thought he recognized someone. Once, he thought he

saw Brian Hoberman coming and ducked into a store.

"Robert, why are you going in here?" his mom asked, following him.

Robert slid the sunglasses down on his nose. He was surrounded by half-naked mannequins wearing ladies' underwear! He ran out again.

"Robert, what is the matter with you?" his mom asked, running to catch up to him. Grandma Judy arrived a moment later, panting.

"Is something wrong?" Grandma Judy asked. She sat down on a bench where she could catch her breath.

"No," said Robert. "I . . . I just made a mistake." He held up the glasses. "It must have been these dark glasses."

"Please stay close to us from now on," said his mom. "Grandma Judy doesn't expect to run through the mall."

Robert remained as hidden from sight as possible until they finally left the mall and drove to Smilin' Jack's.

As always, just walking into the restaurant made Robert feel good. Robert read the posters on the walls. One was a movie poster for *The Wizard of Oz*. Another was for *Frankenstein*.

A woman showed them to a booth with an old-fashioned radio in it. You could press a button and hear a snippet from an old radio program.

"Play one, go ahead," Grandma Judy said.

Robert did. A woman's voice came on saying, "McGee, don't open that closet!" Then a man's voice answered, "It's O.K., Molly, I just want to get my—" and the next thing you heard was a door opening and a lot of stuff crashing down.

Grandma Judy laughed so hard she had to wipe her eyes. It did sound pretty funny.

"You play one," Robert said to Grandma Judy.

With the press of a button came the sound of hoofbeats and music. A voice told about a masked man.

"That's the *Lone Ranger*," Grandma Judy said. "He had an Indian companion named Tonto who called him 'Kemo Sabe.'"

"You remember that?" asked Robert's mom.

"Sure I do," said Grandma Judy. "I remember them all like it was yesterday. *Mr. Keen, Tracer of Lost Persons*. The *Green Hornet*, where they played that buzzy bee music. . . ."

"You mean the 'Flight of the Bumblebee'?" asked Robert's mom.

"Yes, that's it. And *Ellery Queen*. And *Boston Blackie*: 'Enemy to those who make him an enemy; friend to those who have no friend.'"

Robert enjoyed hearing the bits from the old programs and watching Grandma Judy as she remembered.

"It was exciting," she said. "Every night there was a program about good guys going after bad guys."

"What was your favorite?" asked Robert's mom.

"This I remember very well. It was *The FBI in Peace and War*. They had an announcer who talked about Public Enemy #1. Every week they had another story about one of them and how the FBI tracked him down and put him in jail."

Robert put down his Wimpy Burger, named after a comic-strip character. He was no longer hungry. He imagined another poster on the wall, an FBI wanted poster, and underneath it was the notice: GRANDMA JUDY, PUBLIC ENEMY #1.

Keeping the Secret

That night, Robert tried to write his report, but he had trouble getting started. What could he say about how wrong it was to kill animals for their fur when his own grandmother wore a fur coat!

Huckleberry scratched at his pants leg to get his attention. Robert picked him up.

How could she do it? Grandma Judy loved animals. She even brought toys for Huckleberry!

"Mom, can I use the phone?" he called down the stairs to his mom.

"O.K.," she answered, "but don't stay on too long."

Robert put Huckleberry down and dialed Paul's number. He knew it by heart.

"I have to tell you something," he said. "And you have to promise not to tell. It's a secret."

"O.K.," said Paul.

Robert swallowed hard. "My grandmother is a murderer," he said.

"What?" cried Paul. "Get out of here!"

"It's true. She wears a fur coat. The anti-fur people say people who wear fur coats are murderers."

"They also go around spray-painting people who wear fur," said Paul.

"Yes, but they're trying to stop people from killing animals," said Robert. "Like those boats that keep hunters from getting close to the baby seals."

"I don't know," said Paul. "It's good that the baby seals are safe, but ruining someone else's property is wrong, no matter why they do it."

"Yeah. You're right," said Robert. "I liked how mad they got about the animals, though. I even wanted to be one of them."

"You don't have to be one of them," said Paul. "You can do something else."

"Like what?" asked Robert.

"I don't know. We'll think of something," said Paul.

"I . . . I feel so funny now around Grandma Judy," Robert confessed. "It's not the same anymore. I used to love her. . . ."

"You don't love your grandma anymore?" Paul sounded shocked.

"I'm trying not to," said Robert, feeling miserable.

"Why?" asked Paul.

"How can I love someone who does something I hate?"

"I don't know," said Paul, "but you've got to. She's your grandmother."

"I have to go," said Robert. "My mom doesn't want me to stay on the phone too long."

"O.K. See you."

That night, Robert dreamed again about Huckleberry being chased. But this time it was Grandma Judy holding the knife.

Good Publicity

Robert, Emily Asher, Vanessa Nicolini, and Lester Willis were on the floor of Paul's room, where they were all sharing jars of poster paint. Paul sat at his desk, doing his sign in markers.

Emily and Vanessa and Robert had remembered to bring poster board for their signs, but Lester had forgotten. Paul had found a cardboard carton in the basement that Lester was able to tear apart to use for his sign.

Robert looked at his sign. The bright

blue S and T looked pretty good. He made an O, nice and round, then a P.

Robert couldn't help thinking about Grandma Judy as he painted.

He knew the protest was the right thing to do. So why did he feel bad? He guessed it was because he thought he couldn't love Grandma Judy because she did something he didn't like. But that didn't make sense.

Robert stopped painting, right in the middle of a K.

Grandma Judy smoked cigarettes, and he hated that, but he still loved her. Maybe this was like the cigarettes. You could hate something someone does, but that doesn't mean you don't love them.

He went back to his sign.

The protest had grown. Some of the other kids were going, too, if their parents said it was all right. So far Brian, Lester, Vanessa, Emily, Susanne Lee, Paul, and

Robert were planning to go. All they needed now was an adult to go with them.

"I asked my mom," said Paul. "She wasn't sure what she had to do on Saturday, but I think she'll go. She thinks it's a good idea."

"That's great," said Robert. For once, he was glad his mom would be busy. She was taking Grandma Judy into New York to Radio City Music Hall. Grandma Judy loved the Rockettes.

Mrs. Felcher came in. "Popcorn, everyone," she said, looking for a place to set down a big bowl. She moved Paul's books from the top of his bookcase onto his bed and put the bowl there.

Lester got up immediately to grab a handful of popcorn.

"Thanks!" he said, grinning at Mrs. Felcher.

"Oh, those look great," said Mrs. Felcher, looking around the room at the signs.

"Thank you, Mrs. Felcher," said Emily. Her sign, in red letters, read DON'T BE A MURDERER.

Vanessa had painted a picture of a baby seal and her sign, in green, read PLEASE DON'T KILL ME.

"By the way," said Mrs. Felcher, "I'll be able to go with you tomorrow."

"Yay!" yelled Lester, taking more popcorn.

"Double yay!" said Vanessa.

"Cool," said Robert.

"Be sure to tell your parents to call me to let me know it's O.K."

"O.K.," said Robert.

"We will," said Emily and Vanessa at the same time.

Lester just nodded. His mouth was full of popcorn.

"Great. I'll even carry a sign, if you paint one for me," said Mrs. Felcher.

"I'll do it!" cried Vanessa.

"No, me," said Emily.

"I want to do it!" cried Lester.

Mrs. Felcher laughed. "Well, you can fight over me if you want to, just as long as I have a sign to carry."

Robert got up from the floor. His sign was done. He stepped back to look at it. He hadn't left quite enough room at the end so he had to squeeze the letters together for the last word. Still, it looked pretty good.

He swished his paintbrush around in the water until it was clean.

When they were all finished and had cleaned up, they picked up their backpacks and went downstairs to wait for Mr. Dorfman, who was going to drive them home.

At the door, Mrs. Felcher reminded them to have their parents call her. "And be ready at ten o'clock. That's when I'll be by to pick you up."

Robert pulled Paul aside.

"I thought about it," he said. "And I know I can love my grandma after all."

"How come?" asked Paul.

"Because I love my grandma, not her coat."

"Cool," said Paul with a smile.

Robert's dad arrived, and the kids shouted their good-byes as they raced out to the car.

"I wonder if we'll get our names in the newspaper," said Emily as she climbed into the backseat.

"Oh, boy!" shouted Lester Willis, squeezing in next to her. "Wouldn't that be great?"

Robert gulped. He didn't think that would be great at all. What if Grandma Judy picked up the newspaper and read about the protest? Or saw a picture of him carrying his sign?

The Protest

The next morning, Robert avoided questions about what he was doing that day. He took Huckleberry out into the yard to play while his mom and dad and Grandma Judy ate bagels for breakfast.

His mom knew where he was going, but Robert asked her not to tell Grandma Judy. He explained why.

"All right, Robert," said his mom, "but I think you'd be better off telling her."

When Paul and his mom honked the horn, Robert brought Huckleberry back into the house. "Bye!" he shouted as he grabbed his mask and ran out the door to the waiting station wagon.

At the mall, kids were assembled in front of Fancy Furs, carrying their signs.

Brian's sign read FUR COATS MEAN DEAD ANIMALS.

Abby's sign had a drawing of a cute beaver and I HAVE RIGHTS, TOO underneath it.

Vanessa and Emily presented a sign to Mrs. Felcher that she could carry. "We worked on it together," said Vanessa.

"Read it out loud," said Emily.

Mrs. Felcher read her sign. "'NO FAIR, NO FUR.'" She smiled. "I like it. Thank you, girls."

Robert had to laugh at Lester's sign. It was a big picture of Bugs Bunny that Lester must have copied. In a cartoon balloon over his head it read IS THAT MY RELATIVE YOU'RE WEARING?

"Robert!" said Emily. "What a good idea to wear an animal mask."

Robert didn't tell Emily he had only brought it with him to hide his face if somebody took their picture.

A woman stopped to ask them what they were doing. She squinted at Robert's sign. "What does that mean?" she asked. "Stop killing animals to make fur cots? Who makes fur cots?"

"Coats," said Robert. "Fur *coats*." He heard Vanessa giggle behind him.

"Oh," said the lady. She walked on.

A couple of teenage girls walked by.

"Hey," said one of them. "Good for you."

"Look at his mask!" said the other, pointing to Robert. "What are you sup-posed to be?" she asked him.

"A clouded leopard," he answered.

The girl laughed and said, "A clowny leopard? What's that?"

Robert started to correct her, but the first girl cracked up and the second one started laughing, too. They walked off together, laughing so hard they were holding their stomachs.

Children stopped to stare at Robert and his classmates marching in a circle with their signs. Their mothers quickly came and pulled them along.

After a while, a man came out of the store.

"What are you doing?" he cried. "Get away from my store. People won't come in, with you hanging around."

"That's the idea," said Emily, waving her sign at the man.

"I'm calling security," the man said, storming inside.

A few minutes later, a man in a uniform came by, asking what they were up to.

"It's a peaceful demonstration," said Mrs. Felcher. "These children are protesting the wearing of fur."

"Do you have a permit?" asked the security guard.

"I don't believe we need one to walk on public property if we're not causing a disturbance," she answered.

The security guard talked into his walkie-talkie. The store owner came out again, pleading with them to leave. The children kept walking quietly back and forth, carrying their signs.

Robert was feeling a little hot and sweaty under his mask and was thinking of taking it off. Just then, a man came at him with a camera.

"Sonny, hold it right there," he said. *Click!*

The photographer moved from Robert to the others.

Whew! That was close. Robert kept the mask on.

The protest went on for two hours before a policeman came up to Mrs. Felcher and told her they would have to leave. She listened to what he had to say and then, with a shrug, told the children they had to go. She led them out of the building.

"Well, children," she said. "You did a magnificent job. I'm sorry you couldn't stay longer, but it seems the mall has a right to ask you to leave. If you want to protest, you have to stay outside the building."

They looked around. The building was huge.

"And that just won't work," she added. "People won't know what you're protesting. I'm proud of you for coming out today to stand up for what you believe in. You can all go home now feeling good about yourselves."

Mrs. Felcher hung out with them until everyone's ride had come. Finally, they were all accounted for. Robert climbed into the station wagon, happy to take off the mask.

It was a good day. Now, if only Grandma Judy didn't find out about it.

Times Change

It was quiet when Robert came downstairs Sunday morning. His mom and dad were still asleep. He let Huckleberry out the back door to the yard and wandered into the living room.

Grandma Judy was reading the entertainment section of the Sunday paper. "Hi," he said, plopping down on the sofa next to her. The first section of the newspaper lay open on the coffee table. Robert strained to see if there was anything there about the protest.

"Hello," said Grandma Judy with a big smile. "And how are you this morning?"

"Fine," he said.

Grandma Judy said, "That's good," and continued to look at the newspaper.

"No, that's not true," said Robert. Grandma Judy lowered the newspaper and looked up.

"What's not true?" she asked. "You're not fine?"

Robert couldn't bear it any longer. Keeping the secret about Grandma Judy's fur coat from his friends had been bad. Keeping his feelings from Grandma Judy was a lot worse.

"Grandma Judy, I have to tell you something."

"O.K. So tell."

And there, on the sofa, still in his pajamas, Robert told his grandmother everything.

"I'm sorry, Grandma Judy," he said as he

71

finished. His throat almost closed up as he tried not to cry.

"Robert, my love," said Grandma Judy, pulling him to her in a big hug. "You mustn't feel so bad. I understand completely." She stroked his head. "Let me tell you a story." Robert relaxed in Grandma Judy's warm hug.

"From the old days?" he asked.

"Yes, as a matter of fact. From the old days." She smiled and got that look in her eyes that always happened when she talked about Grandpa Aaron.

"It was our 30th wedding anniversary," Grandma Judy said. "Your grandfather, my wonderful Aaron, came home from work with this box. It was a big box. I had no idea what it was. I opened the box. There were roses, lots of roses.

"I took the roses out and pushed the box aside. I was about to get a vase, but Aaron stopped me.

"'No, wait. Look some more,' he said.

"'In the box?' I asked.

"'Where else?' he said. Underneath the tissue paper was a fur coat. It was so soft, so beautiful, I cried.

"'For me?' I asked.

"'Who else?' he said. He was so romantic, your grandfather."

Robert gulped.

Grandma Judy's voice got softer.

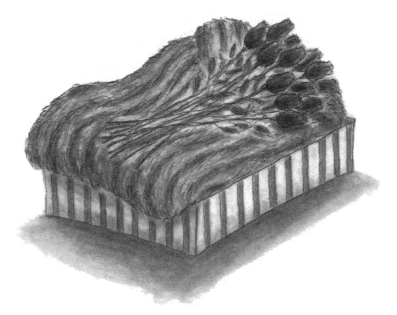

"In those days we didn't think so much about animals—maybe we were too busy worrying about ourselves. Now, everything is animal rights, and people rights, and that's good. Times change. And we should be happy they do."

She squeezed him tight. "But my Aaron, he did something beautiful for me with that coat, and I can't forget that."

For a while, they just sat there like that. It was a beautiful story. Robert wished he had known his grandpa Aaron. He also wished Grandpa Aaron had given Grandma Judy jewelry or something and not a fur coat. Nobody got hurt making jewelry. At least, he didn't think they did.

Grandma Judy was warm and smelled like lilacs. He had missed that wonderful flowery smell that was her. "I'm glad you came to see us, Grandma Judy," he told her.

"Even with my fur coat?" she asked, laughing.

Robert smiled. "Yes. Even with your fur coat."

Later, after tossing a ball to Huckleberry in the yard and playing tug-of-war with his rope toy, Robert went up to his room. Huckleberry curled up on the rug while Robert sat at his desk and wrote his report.

Robert felt a lot better now that he had talked to Grandma Judy. But what would he do about the kids in school? Would they understand if he told them about Grandma Judy's fur coat?

The Report

Robert walked into the classroom and stopped short. There were animals sitting where some of the kids should be.

"Your idea was great," said Emily Asher from under an elephant mask. It had big floppy ears and tusks made from paper towel rollers painted white. Brian had on a buffalo mask with black yarn pasted on for the beard and the head. Vanessa's baby seal mask had big sad eyes.

Paul's was the best. His was a big gray whale. The mask had a little hole in the top, and Paul squirted water through a long tube to make it spout like a sperm whale.

"That's cool," said Robert.

"So is yours," said Paul. "Where did you get those whiskers? You didn't have them at the protest."

"From a broom," Robert answered. "I glued them on last night." Paul laughed.

Robert was glad Paul liked his mask. Paul was the best artist he had ever known. He would know how hard it was to paint all those spots to look like little clouds. Robert had taken his time and had been really careful. He only spilled the jar of black paint once. Luckily, it was on the kitchen table, where it was easy to clean up. His mom hadn't even yelled at him for mopping it up with the souvenir dish towel from Atlantic City. She said she had never liked that towel.

When it was Robert's turn to give his report, he spoke loudly and clearly, so he could be understood through the mask.

"The clouded leopard is very fast," he said, "and a good climber. It can even hang by its back feet from a tree branch."

"No way!" shouted Lester, who never raised his hand before he spoke.

"Way!" said Robert. "It's true. People want its fur to make into coats because it's so unusual," he said. "Now there are only a few left. The clouded leopard is on the endangered list."

Looking around, Robert saw that the kids were moved by his talk. He put down his papers with all his notes. He took off his mask and stood up straight.

"My grandma wears a fur coat," he said. Several kids gasped. Robert swallowed hard.

"She's not a bad person," he said. "She's nice and she's funny. A long time ago, people didn't think about animal rights the way they do now. But times change," said Robert, "and we know better now."

Robert's voice was a little shaky. He cleared his throat.

"I think we have to help the animals on our planet, not kill them. It's up to us to protect them." He collected his papers and took his seat.

"That was a very good report, Robert," said Mrs. Bernthal. "It shows you did your research and learned all about your subject." She turned from Robert to face the whole class.

"I heard about your protest at the mall on Saturday," she said. "The fact that you did something about what you learned is admirable."

Admirable. That meant Mrs. Bernthal admired them! She turned to look at Robert again.

His cheeks felt warm.

He wished he still had the mask on so nobody could see him blushing.

Hello Again

"**R**oll over!"

Huckleberry's tiny tail wagged as he tumbled over at Robert's command. They were just finishing a show of tricks for Grandma Judy.

"Such a smart puppy," she said. "Did you teach him all these tricks, Robert?"

Robert nodded. He was glad that Huckleberry did his newest trick perfectly for Grandma Judy.

Grandma Judy scooped up the puppy. "I'm going to miss you, young fellow," she said, nuzzling the dog's neck.

Her visit was coming to an end. Robert's dad was about to drive her to the airport. He stood there with her luggage as Mrs. Dorfman got Grandma Judy's coat.

"It's time to say good-bye," Grandma Judy said, putting Huckleberry down, "until we say hello again." She wrapped her arms around Charlie and then Robert. "I like to think of it that way so I don't have to dwell on the good-bye part."

"I love you, Grandma Judy," said Robert. "I'm sorry about the fur coat."

Grandma Judy stepped back and looked at him. "Robert, my love, don't think another minute about it," she said. "I am proud that you are such a caring person. I feel safe that you will be in charge of the world one day."

He smiled at the thought of being in charge of anything besides the class library and the class pet and Huckleberry. Wow!

He didn't realize until just then that he was responsible for so much!

Mrs. Dorfman helped her mother into her coat.

"Besides," added Grandma Judy, "I'm thinking—it's time to retire this old coat."

"Really?" said Robert.

"Yes," she replied. "Times change. Fur is not in fashion anymore. I have to get with it and buy myself a new, modern coat.

What do you think of a red one?"

Robert gave her a big hug, smelling her lilac perfume once more.

"Red would be perfect," he told her.

Paul for President!

"**A**nyone home?"

Robert had barely opened the door and called out when Huckleberry galloped up and jumped on him, knocking his book bag to the floor.

Robert knelt down, and the puppy slurped a wet kiss on his nose.

"Huck, how you've grown" said Robert, trying to sound like Grandma Judy. "Soon you'll be taller than me."

It seemed only yesterday that Huckleberry was just a small ball of fur. He had grown so much since Grandma Judy's visit, only a month ago. Robert pushed his face into the dog's warm coat. Huckleberry's tail wagged back and forth.

On days when no one was home after school, Robert was especially glad he had Huckleberry. He knew his mom had to work at her office sometimes, and that once in a while his dad would stay late at school for a teachers' meeting, and that his brother would always be at practice for some sport or another. It didn't happen very often that all three were out at the same time, but Robert had his own key for those times when it did.

Robert got up and went to the kitchen, opened the refrigerator, and stared at the container of milk. Was it fresh? He couldn't be sure unless he smelled it.

He didn't feel like smelling it. If it was
bad, the smell would stay in his nose all
afternoon. He decided to have some juice
instead.

Robert gulped down the juice and put the empty glass in the sink.

"C'mon, boy," he said. As he thumped up to his room, Huckleberry's toenails tap-tapped on the stairs after him.

Robert helped Huckleberry onto his bed and plopped down next to him. "Hey, pal!" He stroked Huckleberry's silky coat. Huckleberry rolled over on his back, his legs in the air. Robert laughed.

"I want a picture of you like that," Robert said, getting up to get his camera.

After taking a couple of good shots, Robert gave the dog a belly rub. Right in the middle of rubbing, he had an idea. He jumped up and went to the phone on the landing outside his room. He dialed Paul's number.

"Paul, I have to take a picture of you," he said.

"O.K. Why?"

"To put on a poster. Kids will see your face and want to vote for you."

Mrs. Bernthal had told them they could hold elections for class president next week. Paul was running for class president, and Robert was his campaign manager.

"They will?" said Paul.

"Yes. They will. You've seen the posters for mayor around town, haven't you?"

"Mostly I just see names."

"Your name will be on a poster like that, but a picture of you will make it even better," said Robert. "They have a machine at the mall that can blow up pictures to poster size. We'll make a copy and put it on poster board. Underneath we'll write in big black letters VOTE FOR PAUL. Then we'll hang it in the hall just outside our classroom. The kids will see it as they walk into the room."

"O.K.," said Paul. "How much will it cost? I already spent most of this week's allowance."

"I have some money," said Robert, remembering Grandma Judy's bingo winnings. "I'll use that."

"Thanks. I'll pay you back next week," said Paul.

"That's O.K.," said Robert. "It's a political contribution."

"Gee, thanks," said Paul. "I'd better wear my new shirt tomorrow."

"Oh. Um . . . I was hoping we could do it today," said Robert.

"I can't today," said Paul. "I have to go to the store with my mom and Nick." Nick was Paul's little brother. "Nick needs new shoes, and he won't try them on for anyone but me.

One more day wouldn't matter. "O.K.," said Robert. He called Huckleberry, and they went downstairs to play ball in the yard.

A New Plan

The next morning, Robert and Paul stared in horror as they walked down the hall to their classroom. Posters with Susanne Lee Rodgers's picture lined the walls. Under each face was the slogan SUSANNE LEE CAN DO THE JOB.

"Oh no!" said Paul. "She beat us to it!"

"Don't worry," said Robert, trying to sound like a good campaign manager. "We'll think of something else."

Paul just shrugged. "It was dumb to think I could win," he said. "Susanne Lee always wins everything." He looked around at the posters and shrugged. "And she's always—there."

"It wasn't dumb," said Robert as they took their seats at Table Four. "You would make a very good class president."

But Robert knew what Paul meant. Susanne Lee was always in your face. That's what bugged him about her.

She always raised her hand first to answer a question or said what you wanted to say before you had a chance to say it.

She volunteered to be a hall monitor before Mrs. Bernthal even said she needed one.

Her homework was always neat and perfect and tacked up on the bulletin board.

It felt like you never had a chance. When did Susanne Lee Rodgers ever sleep?

They had a week to campaign. Jesse Meiner and Emily Asher were also running for class president. Robert had to tell everyone why they should vote for Paul.

"Let's have a meeting at my house this afternoon," said Robert.

"O.K.," said Paul.

Robert didn't know how, but he had to help Paul win this election. His best friend was counting on him.

At Robert's house, Huckleberry met them at the door. The dog danced around, wagging his tail, bringing his chew toy to them.

"What a great welcome!" said Paul.

"Yeah," said Robert. "It's one of the best things about coming home after school. Huckleberry is always happy to see me and ready to play."

In the yard, he and Paul tossed a ball back and forth, challenging Huckleberry to catch it. After Huckleberry ran off with the ball for the third time and he and Paul had to wrestle it away from him, Robert said, "Wait a minute! Don't move!"

He ran into the house and upstairs to his room. He grabbed his camera from his night table. There was still half a roll of film in it. He ran back downstairs and into the yard.

"Stand by the apple tree," he told Paul. Robert snapped a picture. "Now sit on the step." Paul did and smiled into the camera as Robert snapped the next picture.

"I thought it was too late for the poster," said Paul.

"It's still a good idea, so we'll do it," said Robert. "We just have to think of something else, too."

Huckleberry ran by with the ball. Paul grabbed it and tossed it to the dog. Robert needed only one picture of Paul, but he

used up the rest of the film so he could
take it in to be developed right away.

At dinner that night, Robert told everyone
in his family about the campaign.

"That sounds wonderful," said his mom. "Do you have a slogan?" She scooped up something green from a bowl and plopped it onto Robert's plate.

"Um . . . 'Vote for Paul,'" said Robert.

"That's lame," said Charlie. "You need something catchier."

Robert remembered Susanne Lee's slogan: SUSANNE LEE CAN DO THE JOB.

"I know!" said Charlie. "Vote for Paul Felcher, he's a great belcher."

"Charlie!" said Robert's mom.

"That's not funny, Charlie," Robert's dad said. "Let Robert finish."

Robert told them about the posters and how Susanne Lee Rodgers had had the same idea and had beat them to it.

"You can't blame Susanne Lee for using an idea more efficiently than you did," said Mr. Dorfman. "Having a good idea is not enough. It's how you act on it that counts."

"So what are you planning for your campaign?" asked his mom.

Robert circled his fork around the green stuff and dipped into his mashed potatoes. "We're making a poster," he said, "but I have to get a picture of Paul blown up at the mall. Can you take me over there later?"

His dad cleared his throat. "I'll take you, Tiger," he said.

"Thanks, Dad." Robert put his steak bone over the green stuff, hoping no one would notice.

"Watch out for dirty campaign tricks," said Charlie, who seemed to know something about everything. The trouble was, Charlie teased Robert so often, he never knew what to believe and what not to believe.

"What do you mean?" asked Robert.

"You'll see," said Charlie. "Just keep your eyes open."

"I'm glad you're not discouraged by what happened with Susanne Lee," his dad said, "but you have to do more than make a poster."

"I know," said Robert. Robert just didn't have a clue as to what that might be.

At Quik 1-Hour Foto, they dropped off the film. Then they walked around the mall while they waited. They passed a toy store with the latest action figures in the window, a candy shop with multicolored candies of all kinds, and a gazillion clothing stores. They wandered into and out of a sports equipment store, a drugstore, and a bookstore. Finally, they went back for the pictures.

"These are great, Tiger," said his dad, looking through the envelope. "Did you think of this?" He handed the pictures to Robert.

Robert stared at the photo on top. It was a photo of Paul tossing a ball to Huckleberry.

"Vote for Paul—he's on the ball," said his dad, chuckling.

"Thanks, Dad," said Robert. "That's a great slogan!" It was O.K. if his dad came up with the slogan. Maybe the photo was an accident, but he did take the picture, after all.

With the help of a store clerk, Robert used the imaging machine to blow up the photo to a humongous size.

As they paid the clerk, Robert had an idea of his own. "Dad, can we stop at the candy place next?"

"Sure, Tiger."

Robert felt like he was on a roll.

Spying

Before they went into their classroom the next day, Robert and Paul stopped in the hall to hang the poster Robert had made the night before. Susanne Lee's posters were gone. What could have persuaded her to take them down?

The picture of Paul tossing a ball to Huckleberry looked good against the orange-colored poster board he had pasted it on. Underneath it, in huge blue letters, he had printed:

VOTE FOR PAUL— HE'S ON THE BALL!

Later, in the cafeteria, Robert passed around a bag of chocolate-covered peanut butter crunch balls covered in red foil. He held out the bag to Melissa Thurm.

Melissa reached in and pulled out one.

"Vote for Paul—he's on the ball!" Robert said.

"Thanks," said Melissa. She peeled off the wrapper and popped the candy into her mouth.

Lester didn't wait for them to get to his table. He came bouncing up.

"Have one," said Robert. Lester reached in. "Cool," he said, scraping the foil off and slurping up the chocolate-covered ball.

"Vote for Paul—he's on the ball!" said Robert.

"Those peanut butter crunch balls were a great idea," said Paul. "Everyone loves candy."

"Don't think you're so smart, Robert Dorfman!" Robert spun around. Susanne Lee stood there, glaring at him. "You can't give away candy to cover up your sneaky ways."

"What sneaky ways?" Robert asked.

"You know perfectly well what I'm talking about," she said. "You took down all my posters and then put yours up. That was a dirty trick."

Robert was stunned. He never touched Susanne Lee's posters.

"I didn't—" he started to say.

"Just remember, what goes around comes around," she said before she stomped away.

This was terrible. He didn't take down Susanne Lee's posters, but someone did. Who could it be? He remembered Charlie's warning about dirty campaign tricks.

Some of the kids were sucking on peanut butter crunch balls when they got back to the classroom. Mrs. Bernthal quieted the sucking noises by tapping a ruler on her desk.

"I'm happy to see you taking the elections so seriously," she said. "You can campaign during recess and at lunch. In the classroom, we have to do our work. So hurry up and finish your candy and break up into your assigned reading groups."

Robert was glad Mrs. Bernthal didn't make everyone throw their candy into the wastebasket, as she had done once when Lester came in sucking on a jawbreaker.

It was hard to concentrate on reading, and Robert lost his place twice. When he finally got to read, he made only one mistake. He needed help with the word "machine." He forgot that the *ch* could be pronounced like a *sh*.

At lunchtime, Robert noticed Susanne Lee Rodgers, Kristi Mills, Elizabeth Street, and Melissa Thurm whispering to one another. They kept looking at Robert and Paul. Robert wondered if Susanne Lee was telling them all about the posters. He had to know what they were saying.

"I have to do some spying," he announced, getting up from the lunch table. "Wait here."

Robert took his tray and walked the long way around to the trash barrel, passing the girls' table. Maybe he could hear what they were saying. He thought he heard Kristi say something about a platform, but they stopped talking as he walked by. He could tell by the look on her face that

Susanne Lee was still angry.

"Paul, we have to hear what they're say-ing," said Robert, sliding back onto his bench at their table. "I heard something about a platform. That can't be right."

Paul looked over at the girls. He got up to dump his tray. Robert watched as Paul slowed down and spoke to the girls. Kristi said something to him, but Susanne Lee wouldn't even look at him. Paul finished dumping his tray and came back.

"You're right," he said. "They're building a platform."

"Why?" asked Robert. He looked over at the girls. They were leaning over their table and whispering again.

Paul shrugged. "I don't know. They said it's something all the candidates do."

Robert lowered his voice. "Why do you think the girls are building a platform? They could be trying to trick us. They're mad at us for something we didn't do. Charlie said we should be careful."

Paul looked puzzled. "I don't know. Maybe Charlie is right. I never heard about making a platform before. Maybe it's to stand on when you give your speech."

All afternoon they tried to find out more, but the girls weren't talking. It must be pretty important if they were keeping it such a big secret.

Just to be sure, Robert asked Jesse if he had a platform.

"Sure. All the candidates have one. Don't you have yours?"

"Yeah, we do," said Robert. He suddenly felt itchy, just like when he was doing a hard math problem.

"We'd better get working on ours, then," Robert told Paul when they were alone. "Or else I just told a big lie."

The Platform

At Paul's house that afternoon, they searched for lumber. They went down to the basement. Paul's dad sometimes built or repaired things there. They found a couple of boards and scraps of wood, a hammer and nails, and a hot-glue gun.

"This is like playing with blocks again," said Robert.

"Yeah. Except this time we really don't want them to fall down," said Paul.

"How high is a platform?" asked Robert.

"I guess high enough so everyone can see you when you're giving your speech," answered Paul.

They found two long pieces of lumber that looked good for making the base of the platform. They laid the pieces down and put two boards across them. The boards were not the same length. Later, they could saw them even. They hammered the boards to the base.

"It needs to be higher," said Robert. Sure enough, the platform almost disappeared into the grass.

"O.K." Paul picked up some pieces of wood and the hot-glue gun. Gluing one piece to another, he made four stacks of scraps. He glued the stacks to the four corners of the platform, like legs.

They stood back and looked at the platform. It was crooked. One side was higher than the other. Paul used the hot-glue gun

to stick extra pieces of wood to the lower side. That evened out the platform, but when Paul stood on it, it wobbled.

"Whooooa-oo-oa!" he cried, balancing himself. "You have to stand with your feet wide apart so it doesn't wobble."

"O.K.," said Robert. "You can do that."

Paul stared at the platform. "We should even these boards out," he said. He went down to the basement and came back with a saw. He tried to cut the end off the longer board, but the saw blade kept sticking in the wood.

"My dad will kill me if I break his saw," he said, trying to jiggle the saw loose.

"Maybe we'd better leave it alone," said Robert.

"What are we supposed to do with it now?" asked Paul, finally getting the saw out of the wood.

The construction looked more like a raft with feet than a platform.

"I don't know," said Robert. "We'll have to watch what the others do with theirs. Let's keep it in your backyard for now."

"O.K.," said Paul.

They cleaned up the mess they had made in the yard and basement. Afterward, using Paul's art supplies, they cut twenty campaign buttons out of thick paper.

As Robert cut, Paul printed on each of them: VOTE FOR PAUL—HE'S ON THE BALL with a black marker.

By the time Robert went home, his thumb was sore from cutting out all those buttons.

Slogans and Handouts

Before Mrs. Bernthal asked the class to settle down so she could take attendance, Robert and Paul handed out the paper buttons with Paul's slogan printed on them. They also gave each person a safety pin to pin on the button.

Susanne Lee had already handed out long pink strips that had her name written on them with a purple glitter pen.

"Have a bookmark," she said as she handed each kid a strip. "And remember to vote for me. I can do the job." She thrust one at Robert.

Joey Rizzo and Matt Blakey were helping Jesse tape a banner to the wall outside the classroom under the bulletin board. It said, WIN WITH JESSE.

Emily didn't carry a sign or go around or hand out anything. Everyone knew Emily would make a good class president.

Melissa smiled at Paul. "So what about your platform?" she asked. "I haven't heard anything about it." Kristi looked on.

"We have one," said Robert, coming to Paul's rescue. "It's great. It's in Paul's backyard."

"Very funny," said Kristi. "But keeping it a secret is dumb. How will anyone know why they should vote for you? Isn't it time you shared it?"

Robert wasn't sure—was this a trick?

How could they share a platform? They would never all fit. Besides, no one else showed him their platform. They didn't even say where they kept theirs.

At recess, Susanne Lee walked over to Robert and Paul, her hair bouncing.

"So, are you still not telling about your platform?" she said. "It must be pretty bad if you're keeping it a secret." Kristi and Melissa giggled.

"No," said Robert. "It's not a secret. It's a little wobbly, but it's good." He turned to Paul. "Right, Paul?"

"Right," said Paul.

"So what is it?" asked Susanne Lee. She put her hand on her hip.

"You first," said Robert, putting his hand on his hip, too.

"O.K.," said Susanne Lee. She stood as straight as a soldier. "I will start an honor roll for kids with the highest grades."

Robert had a sinking feeling in his stomach.

"I will listen to the problems of anyone in the class and see if I can help solve them," said Susanne Lee.

Robert knew that he must have misunderstood what "platform" meant.

Susanne Lee went on. "As class president, I will help keep the class quiet when Mrs. Bernthal has to leave the room."

Robert and Paul exchanged looks. Paul must have figured it out now, too. He rolled his eyes, making Robert laugh.

Now Susanne Lee put both hands on her hips. "What's so funny?"

"Nothing," said Paul. "I was just thinking . . . about something funny my little brother said." Robert had to struggle not to crack up, thinking of Nick's latest words: "pickle face."

Susanne Lee sighed.

Robert put his hands in his pockets, trying to look cool. "That was very good," he said.

"Well?" demanded Susanne Lee. "What about yours?"

"Oh," said Robert. "We'll have it ready tomorrow."

It wasn't a lie. They would have it ready tomorrow. They just hadn't written it down yet.

Susanne Lee sucked her teeth and walked away. "Pitiful," she muttered.

Robert swallowed hard. That was a close one!

In Your Face

The three o'clock bell rang. Robert and Paul ran two blocks to Paul's house. It was two blocks closer to school than Robert's.

"Hi, boys," said Mrs. Felcher as they flew by her and into the living room.

"Hi!" they shouted back.

"What's the big rush?" Mrs. Felcher asked, following them.

"We have to look something up," said Paul, pulling the dictionary from the bookshelf. He flipped through the pages and stopped. "Platform," he said. He read out

120

loud, "A platform is 'a stage or floor for performers or speakers.'"

"Well, that's what we have," said Robert.

"Wait. There's another meaning," said Paul. "It also says it's 'a statement of principles of a political party.'"

"Oh no!" said Robert. "That's the one they're talking about!"

"It's a good thing we didn't tell them about our platform," said Paul.

"Yeah," said Robert. "They would never stop laughing if they found out."

Paul put the book back on the shelf, and they ran out to the yard.

Robert stared at the platform. He stood on it and rocked. "Whooooa!" he said. "I'm glad you never had to use it. It could make you seasick."

They dragged the platform out into the center of the yard. Paul used the back end of the hammer to try to pry the boards loose.

"I saw my dad do this," he explained. They tugged and pried until their arms hurt. This was even harder than putting the platform together. That platform just didn't want to come apart.

"We have to get it small enough to put out with the trash," said Paul. "My dad is already going to kill me for wasting his lumber. He'd kill me more if I left a mess."

"You always say your dad will kill you," said Robert. "I bet he wouldn't really kill you."

Paul thought about that. "Well, maybe he wouldn't exactly kill me," he said. "But he'd be mad."

"I never saw your dad mad," said Robert. His own father was pretty calm, except when things got out of order. He was a neat freak. Maybe a book would be put back in the wrong place in the bookcase. If he found it, then he'd lecture them on the importance of putting things back where they found them.

"Yeah, my dad doesn't get mad much. I just know he wouldn't like it, though, and that's enough for me." Paul was just like his father. He never got into fights or got really mad at anyone.

At last, they were finished. They went inside to wash up.

"We have to write out our platform," said Paul, soaping his hands in the running water at the bathroom sink.

"Yeah," said Robert, following right behind Paul.

Mrs. Felcher had milk and cookies ready for them when they were cleaned up. They sat down at the kitchen table.

Robert pried open a cookie and licked the cream filling from the inside. Paul got up and tore a piece of paper off the message pad next to the telephone. He took a pencil from the drawer. He put them on the table.

"Let's start," said Paul.

"What would you do as class president?" asked Robert, picking up the pencil.

Paul shrugged. "I don't know," he said. "I've never been a class president before."

"You can make sure everyone does their job, like taking care of the animals." Robert hated it when someone forgot to clean the cages or give the animals food and clean water every day.

"That's good," said Paul. "Our classroom would smell better, too."

Robert wrote it down.

1. MAKE SURE EVERYONE DOES
   THEIR JOB

"You can ask for more class trips," said Robert.

"And more special projects and art supplies," said Paul. He loved to make things and paint.

Robert wrote down:

    2. MORE CLASS TRIPS

    3. MORE SPECIAL PROJECKS

"What about being friendly to new kids?" asked Robert.

"There are no new kids," said Paul.

"But what if we got one?" asked Robert. "We could help them learn about our class and where things are."

"That's good," said Paul. "Write that down."

Robert wrote:

    4. BE HELPFUL TO NEW KIDS

"Susanne Lee said she would do things that would make our class better," said Paul. "We have to think of more things like that."

"These things will make our class better," Robert said.

"It has to be something really important," said Paul.

"Yeah," said Robert, tapping his pencil. "Like making Mrs. Bernthal proud."

"Like keeping Susanne Lee out of our faces," added Paul.

Robert laughed. "We can put her in a suit of armor."

Paul laughed, too. "Or build a portable fence around her that she has to take everywhere with her."

They cracked themselves up. Finally, they stopped laughing.

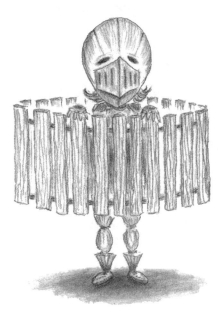

"But she *is* really smart," said Robert.

"I know," said Paul. "But sometimes other kids want to say something. Even if they're not always right, they should get a chance."

There was a pause.

"I know," said Paul. "I will make a rule that no one can raise their hand all the time."

"Can you do that?" asked Robert.

"I don't know," said Paul. "I'll try."

They worked at writing it down until it came out just right. Robert read it back.

5. MAKE SURE EVERYONE GETS A CHANSE

It sounded good. Now, Paul had to write his speech. He had to convince his classmates that he was the best person for the job.

Three Different Beginnings

It was Saturday, and Paul was still working on his speech.

Robert could hardly sit still. He called Paul.

"Hi," he said. "How is the speech going?"

"It's hard. Whenever I say something about what I will do as class president, it sounds like I'm bragging."

"Yeah. Susanne Lee has no trouble doing that."

"Exactly. Maybe she should be class president because she doesn't mind being pushy." Paul sounded discouraged.

"Why don't you come over and we'll work on it together?" said Robert. "We can also take some time out to play with Huckleberry. He needs some exercise."

"O.K.," said Paul. "I'll bring what I have so far."

"Good."

Paul arrived with a large envelope. He took out several pages and made three piles. "This is my speech," he said.

"What are the three piles?" asked Robert.

"Well, it's one speech, but there are three different ways to begin it."

"Wow." Robert had no idea how difficult it was to write a speech. "Why don't you read all of them. Then we can choose the best one."

There was a knock on the door. "Hi,

boys," said Mrs. Dorfman. "Would you like to have dinner with us tonight, Paul?"

Robert looked at Paul. That would be great! Dinner wouldn't be as good as dinner at the Felchers, but it would be fun, anyway.

"We're going to have take-out Chinese food tonight," added his mom, as if reading his mind.

"Yes!" said Robert. It was getting even better. His mom wasn't cooking.

"Sure," said Paul. "Thanks. I'll have to call my mom."

Paul made his phone call, and Mrs. Felcher said it would be fine. Then Mrs. Dorfman took the phone from Paul.

"My husband will drive Paul home," she promised.

Robert looked at Paul. "Limousine service," he whispered. Paul nodded and smiled.

They went back to working on Paul's

speech. Huckleberry lay across the bed on his back, all four paws in the air, fast asleep.

"He's smiling," said Paul.

"Yeah. He smiles," said Robert. "Pepperoni smiled, too. People say dogs don't smile, but I know two dogs who do." Pepperoni was Huckleberry's father. Robert had once trained him to be adoptable, for the Animal Shelter. That was before Robert's parents let him have a dog of his own.

Paul read the first speech out loud. *"As your class president, I want to make sure everyone in our class is treated fair and square."*

Robert applauded as Paul finished. "That's good," he said.

Paul read the second version.

"You know how it is when you have something to say and you don't get a chance to say it?" he began.

Robert couldn't believe it. The first one was good, but the second beginning was even better.

"O.K., here goes," said Paul, reading from the third set of papers.

"What you have to say matters." He went on. Robert was mesmerized.

This one was even better than the first two. Wait a minute. He needed to hear the first one again. And maybe the second.

"They all sound good," said Robert.

"See what I mean?" said Paul.

It was hard deciding which one to use. "Bring them downstairs when we have dinner. My family can help us decide."

"O.K.," said Paul, clipping together the three sets of pages and slipping them back into the envelope.

Huckleberry Votes

Huckleberry woke up and started prancing around the room.

"Huckleberry wants to go out," said Robert. "Come on. We'll play catch with him."

They thumped down the stairs, one after the other, Huckleberry click-clicking in the lead.

It was good to be out in the crisp November air. There were still a few leaves on the apple tree, but most of them were in a pile on the side of the yard. Huckleberry loved running into the leaves after

the ball. Before long, all three of them were diving into the leaves.

Mrs. Dorfman called them in for dinner. They were glad to come in and get warm. Robert led Paul to the bathroom, where they washed up.

When they sat down at the table, Robert was glad not to see the usual fish sticks or chicken nuggets.

There were several large bowls set out. One contained shrimp and vegetables, another had sliced up beef and broccoli, another had chunks of chicken with sesame seeds on them, and another had steaming rice.

In smaller bowls were crispy noodles and fortune cookies. All the smells made Robert's nose twitch happily.

"Dig in," said Mr. Dorfman.

The food tasted as good as it looked.

"We never have Chinese food at our house," said Paul. "This is great."

Robert had eaten at Paul's house lots of times. Paul's mom made great food. It was nice to know his own mom could have great food, too, even if she didn't cook it herself.

As the dishes were cleared from the table, Robert asked Paul to take out his speech. Everyone hung around to hear it, except for Charlie.

"My friends will be here to pick me up in ten minutes," he said. "I have to go." It was Saturday night. Nobody expected Charlie to stay home.

"Be home by eleven," Mrs. Dorfman reminded him.

Charlie grunted, said "O.K.," and left.

Mr. and Mrs. Dorfman pulled their chairs back from the table and sat, listening. "The floor is yours," said Mr. Dorfman.

"This is Number One," Paul began. "It's the first one I wrote." Nervously, he looked around. He cleared his throat and began.

"As your class president. I want to make sure everyone in our class is treated fair and square. . . ."

When Paul finished his whole speech, everyone applauded, and Huckleberry wagged his tail.

"Just one thing," said Mr. Dorfman, still clapping. "It's a very good speech, but you should say 'fairly and squarely,' not 'fair and square.'"

"Oh. Fairly and squarely," repeated Paul. "Thanks."

Paul picked up another set of papers. "Number Two," he announced. "This one is like I'm talking to a friend. I thought it might sound better that way." He began.

"You know how it is when you have something to say and you don't get a chance to say it? . . ."

There was another round of applause and a tail wag when he finished.

"Then," said Paul, "after I wrote the others, I thought maybe it should sound more important and be stronger. So I wrote this." Paul read version Number Three.

"What you have to say matters! . . ."

There was more clapping as Paul put his papers down and took a small bow.

Huckleberry stood up, wagging his tail.

"O.K.," said Robert. "We have to vote on which speech Paul should give tomorrow. Raise your hand for Number One."

Mr. Dorfman raised his hand. "That was an excellent speech, Paul," he said. "You told your classmates what you planned to do and why you felt it was important."

Robert wrote under Speech #1: 1

"How many votes for the second one?" he asked. His mom raised her hand.

"I liked the friendly way you got the kids to think about what it's like to be left out," she said.

Robert wrote under Speech #2 : 1

"Number Three?" he asked. Robert raised his own hand.

He wrote under Speech #3: 1

"Paul, how do you vote?"

"I don't know. That's my problem. I can't decide." Paul looked worried.

Huckleberry wagged his tail furiously.

"We have a tie," said Robert. He looked at Huckleberry. "Come here, boy."

Huckleberry went up to Robert and sat, obediently.

"Good boy. Now stay here," Robert commanded. He gave the papers for Speech Number One to his dad, handed those for Speech Number Two to his mom, and gave the last set, for Speech Number Three, to Paul.

"Now, when I say 'go,' each of you call Huckleberry. The one he goes to has the speech he votes for."

All three went into the living room and lined up with their speeches in hand. Robert took Huck to the other end of the room. At the signal, there was a commotion of sounds and motions.

"Come!" Mrs. Dorfman bent over and made baby sounds.

"Here boy, this way, come on." Mr. Dorfman used his deepest voice.

"Aw, Huckleberry, c'mon over here." Paul waved the speech as though it were a toy.

"Huck, Huck, attaboy, come here."

"Hey, boy, come to me."

"Huckleberry, come!"

"C'mon, boy!"

"Huckleberry! Here!"

"Here, sweetie, come to Mama."

Huckleberry did not know which way to turn, but at last he walked over and sat at Paul's feet.

Robert shouted. "Huckleberry voted!" he cried. "It's Speech Number Three!"

Promises

Jesse, Joey, and Matt did not look happy on Monday morning. They stared at Robert and Paul as they walked into the classroom.

"What's going on?" Robert asked Vanessa, who sat at Table Four with them.

"Their banner is gone," said Vanessa. "They think you took it."

"What? Why do they think that?" said Robert.

"Because you took down Susanne Lee's posters," said Vanessa.

"We did not!" shouted Robert. "We didn't take down any posters or banner!"

The other kids just stared back at them. What could they do? Everyone believed they did it. That certainly wouldn't win Paul any votes.

Mrs. Bernthal took the attendance. "Excellent!" she said when she knew everyone was there.

"Today, class," she said, "we will hear some speeches. Will the candidates for class president please come up front?"

Emily, Jesse, Susanne Lee, and Paul went up and stood in front of Mrs. Bernthal's desk.

Mrs. Bernthal complimented them on their campaigns. "You ran good campaigns," she said. Mrs. Bernthal didn't say anything about the missing posters and banner.

"And no matter who gets the most votes, you are all winners to me," she said.

Jesse and Susanne Lee stared at Robert and Paul.

It wasn't fair. The other kids thought Robert and Paul did something wrong that they didn't do.

"May the best person win," Mrs. Bernthal said.

Emily went first.

"If I am elected class president," she began, "I promise to see that the girls are included in all the sports that the boys are—softball, basketball, running, etcetera." She paused. Then she added, "And I promise that boys will have to jump rope and be cheerleaders."

The boys gasped. The girls clapped. Someone even whistled.

Emily continued her speech and concluded with, "And so a vote for Emily is a vote for equal rights."

All the girls applauded vigorously. The

boys just sat and stared.

"Thank you, Emily," said Mrs. Bernthal. "Jesse, you're next."

Jesse was wearing a suit and tie. He never missed a chance to show that he was cool. He promised that he would ask Mrs. Bernthal for more science projects. He promised he would work for a class trip to the Liberty Science Museum. He promised that he would do something about stolen lunches and fighting on the playground.

After Jesse, Susanne Lee came forward. Her hair bounced with every step she took. She wore big, pink hair bows.

Susanne Lee promised the class they would have 100 percent attendance every day. Robert imagined her pulling sick kids out of bed to drag them to school.

Susanne Lee promised to help kids who had problems with their math and spelling and reading. Robert gritted his teeth as she talked. He remembered sitting in a reading group with bossy Susanne Lee as the leader.

"As class president," Susanne Lee said, "I promise to see that our class behaves when Mrs. Bernthal leaves the room."

The boys groaned.

Paul was up last, wearing his favorite shirt and his "rocket pocket" jeans. He had

painted rocket ships on the back pockets of his jeans.

Robert had listened to Paul's speech a gazillion times, so he knew it by heart. He almost held his breath until it was over. Paul did not make any mistakes.

Paul finished with Robert's favorite line, *"It's not what we say today that matters, but what we do tomorrow."* That was the line they worked on the most together. They had added "today" and "tomorrow" at the very last minute.

All the speeches were good. It was impossible to guess who would win. The boys probably wouldn't vote for Emily, but a lot of girls would. Would the class believe all the promises that were made? Would anyone vote for Paul? It was going to be torture for Robert waiting for tomorrow to come.

Election Day

Mrs. Bernthal showed them how to use their ballot to vote.

"There is a list of the candidates' names." She held up a piece of paper. "In front of each name is a little box. Put a check mark next to the name of the person you are voting for. Then fold the paper in half like this," she said as she showed them, "and put it in the box on my desk." Mrs. Bernthal pointed to a cardboard carton with BALLOTS printed in black marker on the side.

"Can we vote twice?" shouted Lester Willis.

"You will get only one ballot," Mrs. Bernthal answered. "And you may check off only one name. If there are multiple check marks, the ballot will be voided." Robert liked the way Mrs. Bernthal talked to them as though they were grownups.

"I will count the ballots," said Mrs. Bernthal, "and I will announce the winner."

When everyone had deposited their ballots in the box, Mrs. Bernthal picked up the box and shook it. She took the lid off and began counting votes at her desk.

After slowly and carefully taking out each paper, Mrs. Bernthal read it and put it in a pile. Robert watched as she put one paper in one pile, two in the next, one in the next, and so on.

There were four piles. When the box was empty, she counted each pile.

"Your class president is . . . Susanne Lee," said Mrs. Bernthal.

Robert let his breath out. He looked at Paul. Paul didn't look upset.

"This is how the voting went," said Mrs.

Bernthal, going up to the chalkboard. She picked up a piece of chalk and wrote:

Susanne Lee 7
Paul Felcher 6
Jesse Meiner 4
Emily Asher 3

Robert's eyebrows went up. He looked over at Paul. Paul's mouth was open. It looked like he was saying, "Wow," but without any sound coming out.

Once the results of the election were announced, Mrs. Bernthal asked them to work on their special projects. They were studying Native Americans. Robert was constructing a pueblo out of papier mâché. Paul was in the back of the room, painting a miniature tepee.

Robert walked over to see the tepee. Paul had painted a running deer on it.

Vanessa, sitting nearby, was making a pot with coils of clay.

"Congratulations," she said to Paul. "You almost won."

"Thanks," said Paul.

"That's true," said Robert, turning to Paul. "Susanne Lee had only one vote more than you."

"Yeah. That must mean the kids didn't really think we took down Susanne Lee's posters and Jesse's banner." Paul grinned.

"We had a good campaign," Robert said. "It must have been our platform."

That cracked them up. Paul laughed so hard his paintbrush spattered one of the horses he was painting. Vanessa just stared at him.

"It's a spotted pony," Paul told her.

That did it. Robert laughed so hard he had to go to the bathroom. He got the hall pass from Mrs. Bernthal and ran out the door.

Lester Willis was in the boys' bathroom when Robert got there. He was still wearing his VOTE FOR PAUL—HE'S ON THE BALL button.

"Yo! Robert!" he greeted him.

Robert never knew what to expect from Lester. He had been bullied by Lester once, but that had changed. They were not exactly friends, but Lester didn't bother him anymore. He even acted like he liked Robert sometimes.

"Hi, Lester," he said, doing what he came to do.

"How'd you like those elections?" Lester asked.

"They turned out great," Robert answered. He added, "We almost won."

"Yeah," said Lester with a big grin on his face. "I wanted you to win."

"Thanks." Robert went over to the sink to wash his hands.

"I should have done more stuff to help," said Lester.

"What do you mean?" asked Robert.

"You know . . . like the posters and things," said Lester.

"What about the posters and things?"

Lester grinned again. "Wasn't it funny how they kept disappearing, all except yours?"

Robert dried his hands in a hurry. He was afraid of what Lester was about to say. "You mean . . . you . . . ?" He couldn't finish his sentence.

"I had to," said Lester. "I wanted you guys to win."

Robert couldn't speak. What could he

say? He certainly couldn't say thank you for doing something like that.

"I . . . I . . . have to get back," he said. He forced a smile.

"O.K. See you later," said Lester.

Robert raced back to the classroom and told Paul.

"It's a good thing we didn't win," said Paul. "That would be like stealing."

"Yeah," said Robert. "It probably wouldn't even count. We'd have to do it over."

"Really?" said Paul.

"Charlie says there are lots of dirty tricks during elections." Robert watched Paul paint a zigzag design around the top of the tepee. "But that's not the way I'd want to win."

"Yeah, me neither." Paul painted his last zig.

There was a long quiet moment.

"We'd better talk to Lester," said Robert.

"Yeah," said Paul, putting down his paintbrush. "We can't let him think he did a good thing."

Dirty Tricks

"Hey, Lester, can we talk to you?" said Robert, walking up to Lester's table. Paul was right beside him.

Lester looked up from the clay pot he was making. "Yo, guys. What's up?"

"It's about the elections," said Paul.

"Cool, huh? You almost won."

"Um, Lester," said Robert, "that's what we want to talk to you about. We know you wanted us to win . . . but . . . well . . . we didn't want to win that way."

160

Lester looked blank. "Huh? What do you mean? What way?"

"By playing dirty tricks on the other candidates," said Paul. "We only want to win because the kids think we can do the best job."

Butterflies flew around in Robert's stomach. He couldn't help remembering the fight he once had with Lester. Lester had almost smothered him by sitting on him.

Lester's forehead wrinkled. "I just wanted to help," he said.

"Yeah, I know," said Robert. "And we're glad you were on our side. But we aren't glad that now some of the kids think we're . . ."

". . . sneaky," said Paul. "If people think we took down their posters, they would never trust us on anything ever again."

Lester didn't get mad. He just looked puzzled. Robert felt sorry for him.

Suddenly, Lester pushed his chair back and got up. He walked over to Table 3.

"Yo, Susanne Lee!" he said. "I took down your posters."

"Oh, really?" Susanne Lee shouted back at Lester. She stood up to face him. "So they asked you to do their dirty work, did they? You're pitiful, Lester Willis! You're all pitiful!"

"No!" said Lester, even louder. "They didn't ask me. I just did it. I didn't want you to win."

Susanne Lee looked surprised and sat back down.

By now, Mrs. Bernthal was interested. "May I ask what's going on?" she asked.

"Nothing," said Lester. "I just had something to tell Susanne Lee."

"Well, good," said Mrs. Bernthal. "Perhaps we can say what we have to a little more quietly."

Lester went back to Table 5 and sat
down.

"Thanks," said Robert, letting out his
breath finally. Lester nodded as he

slapped a piece of clay in his hands and continued to work on his pot.

Wow. Robert never knew Lester was so brave. It wasn't just confessing. He had stood up to Susanne Lee!

Everybody Listened

Huckleberry met Robert and Paul at the door. Nobody else was home. Robert's mom worked at the travel agency on Tuesdays. Robert wished someone was home so he could tell them all about the elections.

"Hey, Huckleberry," said Robert, dropping his book bag. "We almost won!" He scratched the dog behind his ears.

Huckleberry broke away from Robert, went racing into the other room, and came back with the cloth doll. He dropped it at Paul's feet.

"Your victory present," said Robert. "He takes out his stinkiest toys for special occasions."

Paul dropped his book bag on the floor and reached for the doll. "Yuck!" said Paul, touching it. "It's gross!"

"I told you," said Robert. "He loves that thing and slobbers all over it."

Paul made a face as he tried to play tug-of-war with the disgusting doll.

"Hey, Huck, let's go outside," he said. The dog dropped the toy and ran for the door. "It worked!" said Paul.

In the yard, Robert picked up Huckleberry's ball and tossed it to Paul.

"I came close to being class president," said Paul to Huckleberry. "And you helped. You chose my speech." Huckleberry grabbed the ball and ran around the yard with it.

"You know," said Paul, watching Huckleberry run, "I still can't believe so many kids voted for me."

Robert sat on the swing and pushed a little. "I can't believe Lester Willis told everyone what he did."

"Yeah," said Paul. "I think he finally got it—that winning fair is the only way to win."

"You know the best thing?" said Paul. "Everybody listened to what we had to say. Even Susanne Lee. So maybe she'll think about giving everybody else a chance."

"Yeah. That's right," said Robert. "Maybe now Susanne Lee will not win every single contest and get every word right on her spelling tests, too."

"And next time, when Mrs. Bernthal asks a question, she won't be the first one to throw up her hand to answer."

There was a pause. Huckleberry came over and sat down, staring at Paul, then at Robert. Paul looked at Robert. Robert looked at Paul.

"It'll NEVER HAPPEN!" they said at the same time.

Collapsing in the grass, they laughed so hard they could hardly get up. They loved cracking themselves up.